HAMTARO, PRIVATE EYE

Adapted by Frances Ann Ladd
Illustrated by Robin Cuddy

SCHOLASTIC INC.

New York   Toronto   London   Auckland   Sydney
Mexico City   New Delhi   Hong Kong   Buenos Aires

ISBN 0-439-53964-1

Published by Scholastic Inc.
SCHOLASTIC and associated logos are trademarks and/or registered trademarks of Scholastic Inc.

Cover design by Peter Koblish
Interior design by Bethany Dixon

12 11 10 9 8 7 6 5 4 3 2 1   4 5 6 7 8/0

Printed in the U.S.A.
First printing, April 2004

"Hamha!" said Hamtaro.
"How are you?"
"Not good," said Oxnard.
"Bijou lost her jewelry box!"
"I'm so sorry," said Hamtaro.

"Quick!" called Boss.
"You better come inside!"

"My book is gone!" said Maxwell.
"My extra apron!" said Howdy.

"Let's solve this mystery!"
said Hamtaro.
"What if the thief is one of us?"
asked Stan.
"Who hasn't had anything stolen?"

"But that's me!" said Hamtaro.
"You think I'm the thief?"
"It couldn't be!" said Boss.
"Hamtaro would never steal.
Let's all look again."

"I've looked everywhere,"
said Boss.
"What's this doing here?"
"That's what I'd like to know!"
said Maxwell.

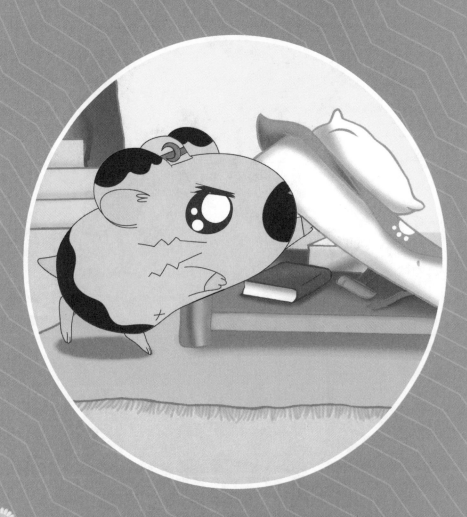

"Who's the best Ham-Detective!"
Hamtaro sang.
"Hamtaro, come back to the
clubhouse," said Oxnard.
"Did you find something?"
Hamtaro asked.
"Kind of," said Oxnard.
"Come on!"

"My jewelry box!" said Bijou.
"My book!" said Maxwell.
"My apron!" said Howdy.
"Our stuff has been found,"
said Dexter.

"Case closed," said Stan.
"The proof is right here!"
"Are you calling me a thief?"
asked Boss.
"Who else?" said Stan.
"That's it!" said Boss.
"I'm leaving!"

"Boss stood up for me.
Now I'll stand up for him.
Boss is not a thief," said Hamtaro.
Boom, Boom, Boom!
"What's that?" cried Howdy.
"A tunnel monster!" cried Oxnard.
"It must be the thief!" said Hamtaro.
"Let's catch him!"

Boom, Boom, Boom!
"The tunnel is shaking!
It's coming closer!"
said Boss.

"Penelope!" cried Boss.
"Ookyoo!" said Penelope.
"You are the thief!" said Boss.
"Ookyoo!" said Penelope.

The Ham-Hams raced into Boss's room.
"Penelope is the thief!" said Boss.
"But she's just a baby!" said Bijou.
"A baby who copies what we do!"
said Maxwell.
"Hasn't she seen you hide
treats under your bed?"

"I knew it was Penelope!"
said Hamtaro.
"Ookyoo!" said Penelope.
"Stop, thief!" said Oxnard.
"That's my seed!"

"I think we all learned a lesson,"
said Hamtaro.
"To keep an eye on our stuff?"
said Oxnard.

"No!" said Hamtaro.
"We have to trust one another!"